Life's Little
Fable

Life's Little Fable

PATRICIA CORNWELL

illustrated by Barbara Leonard Gibson

G. P. PUTNAM'S SONS   NEW YORK

G. P. Putnam's Sons, a division of Penguin Putnam Books for Young Readers,

345 Hudson Street, New York, NY 10014.

G. P. Putnam's Sons, Reg. U.S. Pat. & Tm. Off.

Published simultaneously in Canada

Printed in Hong Kong by South China Printing Co. (1988) Ltd

Text set in Weiss

Library of Congress Cataloging-in-Publication Data

Cornwell, Patricia Daniels.

Life's little fable / Patricia Cornwell; illustrated by Barbara Leonard Gibson.

p. cm. Summary: In the land of pond there is no gravity and Jarrod, who has never fallen or felt heavy

or learned to swim, wants to go into the pond, not knowing the grave danger that lurks there.

[1. Gravity—Fiction.] I. Gibson, Barbara, ill. II. Title.

PZ7.C81647Li 1999 [E]—DC21 98-3669 CIP AC

ISBN 0-399-23316-4

1 3 5 7 9 10 8 6 4 2

First Impression

To my mom

ong ago in the land of the pond, where the sun shone bright and days were long, there lived a boy named Jarrod. He had a sister and a mother and a house made of straw on a side of the forest where people were poorest.

But sunlight did not make dark places called shadows in the land of the pond, and children could climb trees all day long and never fall from branch or frond. Jarrod knew, because he was daring and didn't like rules. Strapping a wooden knife to his side, barefoot and in shorts made of tiger hide, he would climb anything he pleased and play *War* and *Where Am I?* and *Got There First* with his friends. They would fly and fling through the air with never a care, as if they belonged there, like birds.

It did not occur to Jarrod that in places far away from where he lived and played, people suffered from a heaviness called gravity. His mother had not told him yet that beyond the forest the ground grabbed people and held them down, and leaves and clouds stole the sun whenever they pleased, not sharing or caring what might freeze. Days were hard far away across the seas, and people fell from the heaviness and shadows fell from trees.

But Jarrod never gave a thought to what his mother said. He climbed tall pines and took naps in palms, and perched in wooden arms so high above the ground that birds talked about him with each other. They flapped and complained, making angry sounds, for they did not like the people of the pond or want them around. Only birds should dip and spin and spy from the air, and they would squawk to each other that it wasn't fair.

On Saturdays, when Jarrod was not in school, he swung from a long rope tied
to a very tall oak at the edge of the pond crystal blue. Like him, it was small.
But no one knew how deep. Jarrod had asked his mother many times.

    "What would happen," he would say on a day when he was bored, "if
I soared from the sky into that watery world? How far down would I fly?"
he would ask, for he did not know about falling.

His mother was most upset with this, for she knew the pond was a terrible abyss, where there lived a cruel god with gills like a fish.

She warned her son, "Everywhere else you may soar and sail, sing and skip, and never trip or fail. But do not go near the pond."

"Why can't I?" he argued. "I am more than seven, and tired of playing in the heavens. I want to swing over the pond and fly into it like a stone. If it makes you feel better, I won't do it alone. Jenny, like me, is getting tired of trees."

She was his older sister, and though he didn't know exactly, he stated matter-of-factly that she was "more than ten."

In despair Jarrod's mother ran her fingers through her hair and could not keep the truth from him any longer.

"Your father was just like you, only bigger and stronger," she said, sitting Jarrod on her knee. "He, too, got curious about the pond, and sat on the edge of it, tossing stones and counting ripples and rings and imagining all sorts of things about a heaviness he had heard of and trees that paint darkness on the ground."

"Where is he now?" Jarrod sadly asked as he had many times in the past.

"He is where people go when they fall," his mother said.

"What is fall?" He scratched his head.

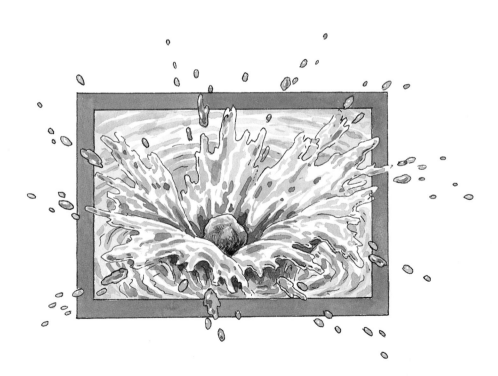

"In the land beyond the pond, trees blaze and go out like fire, and leaves turn brown and fall, floating down. People steal light. They do not share it. I would never live there. I could not bear it," she tried to explain.

But her meaning wasn't plain, and he repeated, "Like a leaf? They turn brown and fall to the ground?"

"In a manner of speaking, when people are seeking only themselves. The heaviness takes them over as they cast a darkness in their shape that follows them wherever they go. This is what happens to people who listen to the god of the pond," she stated.

Jarrod climbed down from her knee. "Who is he?" he wanted to know. "And what did he do with my father?"

He held his mother in his wide blue stare, and thought nothing she had said was fair.

"Your father is in the fallen place, just like most of the human race," she was sorry to tell her son. "I'm afraid he got all too fond of tossing stones in the pond—and listening to the god whisper in tiny splashes of water."

"What did he say?" Jarrod could barely wait, for he wanted to hear them too.

"'Come in and play,'" his mother quoted. "'I am liquid sapphire, cool and hot. I am everything you are and everything you're not. I will give you more until you have nothing, and others will worship you until you're alone. Toss yourself in like a stone, and I will spread your power as you sink down into the darkness where I sit on my throne.'"

"And did he?" he was entranced. "My father must have been very brave and strong to take such a chance?"

Jarrod did not know he could not breathe water, and had never been told the pond had no bottom. He could not imagine a throne or anyone sitting on it in a deep dark wetness like that, and he did not understand sinking, for he had not discovered the heaviness yet.

Saturday came and storm clouds reminded Jarrod of his mother wringing her hands. He carved a walking stick and picked his way through the woods, his head full of plans. Fear was a drop of cold water rolling over his heart, and when he got to the pond he did not know where to start. Should he call out to see if anyone was there, touch his finger to clear blue water, did he dare?

"Who are you?" a voice suddenly bubbled up from the deep, and Jarrod was so startled, for a moment he could not speak. "Answer, little boy," said the god of the pond, making a gurgling, guttural sound, loud enough to be heard all around.

"I am Jarrod," he managed to squeak, while birds in the air pointed their beaks and shrieked, flapping and wheeling, swooping and looping around the pond. They knew very well what lurked deep down, and hoped that the boy of the trees would get weak in the knees and fall and find out for himself, like others.

"Jump in, jump in, the water feels fine!"screamed the birds every time, in words that sounded like banging chimes and broken jars. Turtles, catfish, bream and bass joined in as the god of the pond bubbled up other promises to him.

"Wade in just an inch or two, and this is what I promise to do," his strange sounds bubbled and boiled. "I will make your sister give you her toys, and you can take whatever you want from the store. You will never have to pay or do another chore. As for school, who cares about that? I never went, and I'm smart and fat. You can be like me, little man," said the god, and Jarrod almost ran.

He was shaking, and his voice squeaked when he tried to speak. "I just want to play every day and find my father," he tried to say. "I want to be big so I don't have to listen to my mother."

"Bring me your sister, you won't even miss her," said bubbles breaking into the air as eyes began to glow like fire down there. "Your size seems fine to me. What about your sister, how plump is she? Come to me and you will see what heaviness is like and how it feels to live with no warmth or light, in a world where you don't have to get up until night. You can be a god like me."

Jarrod thought about his mother, and his sister. He stepped closer to the water, watching bubbles as he thought about the trouble he would cause at home. He stepped closer yet, and the eyes burned brighter as his toes got wet.

"Come in." The voice told him what to do. "I was once a little boy, too. Think how powerful you can become. Why, a glimpse of you will make people run. Swim closer, my friend, and we'll have fun."

But Jarrod would not as he watched the god, whose eyes blazed back. Animals, fish and birds all seemed so excited for him to be invited into the pond, and he wondered why. He thought about what his mother had told him, and was about to cry as the eyes got closer, like two yellow moons, while creatures screeched and sang the same, rude tune. Jarrod thought he saw two small caves rise out of the water, and they turned into a snout attached to teeth that made him shout and shudder.

The jaws opened wide, but no matter how hard Jarrod tried, he could not run. He felt heavy like rocks and stuck in gum. The mouth gaped, baring long yellow teeth and a thick red tongue, as he slipped and splashed, screaming at the top of his lungs.

The god of the pond was green like slime, a big ugly crocodile as old as time. He was so close Jarrod could smell foul breath and death, and he jammed his walking stick into that mouth. The so-called god was stuck like a mouse, green tail thrashing and splashing as he tried to spit it out.

"You liar!" Jarrod screamed from the bank as fiery eyes went out. "I don't want to be like you and turn ugly and cold and do nothing but chew! And all you birds and fish can be quiet, too. From now on, the god of the pond is me and you."

There was silence in the forest that day as the crocodile finally went away.
He slid down deep, where he would never again sleep or make another peep
or dream evil schemes. The people of the pond learned to swim and make
boats, while birds discovered they could float. All of them were friends.

The End.